HOCKEY
WARS 3
THE TOURNAMENT

SAM LAWRENCE & BEN JACKSON
ILLUSTRATOR KYLE FLEMING

www.indiepublishinggroup.com

It's not necessarily the amount of time you spend at practice that counts; it's what you put into the practice.

—Eric Lindros

OTHER BOOKS BY SAM & BEN

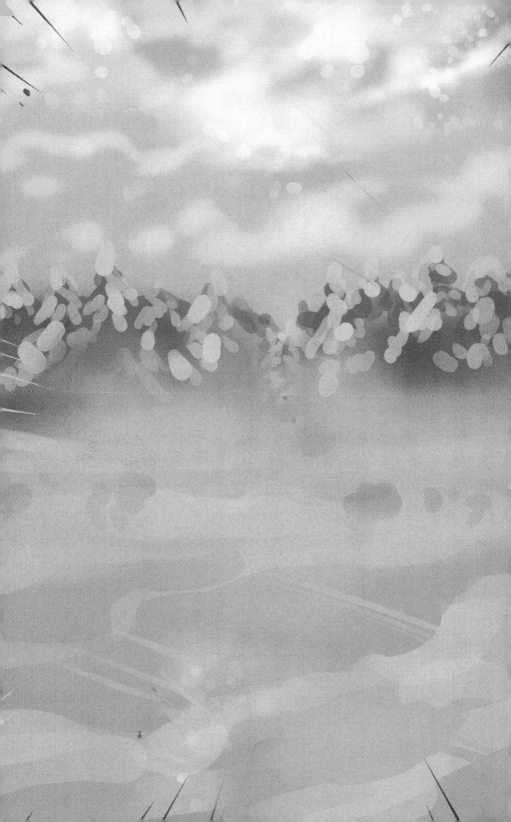

"ALL RIGHT, EVERYONE! A bit of quiet!" Coach John shouted across the bus. Coach John had been coaching the boys' hockey team, the Dakota Lightning, for several years now but knew most of the boys and girls from both teams. "I know you're excited for our first away tournament of the season, but I have to get the rules out of the way. Who knows the rules and wants to help me out? Cam? Millie?"

1. No messing around on the bus and throwing stuff while we're driving.

2. No messing about in the hotel after the coach calls lights out.

3. Between games, it's time to relax and rest for the next game, but at the end of the day, it's time for fun.

4. Most importantly, represent the Dakota Hurricanes and Dakota Lightning, but have fun and don't forget where you come from!

Cameron and Millie took turns shouting out the rules. They knew them all by heart, but some of the other kids hadn't been away on tournaments, so it was all new for them. Millie was the girls' captain and Cameron was the boys' captain. They used to play together when they were younger, but as they got older, they split into boys' and girls' teams.

Initially, this had led to a lot of drama, especially as they were best friends. It had all come to a head the year before, but a grudge match had sorted it out, and now they were closer than they had ever been.

"Thanks, you two! That's right. Play hard, but remember, we're all representing our teams." Coach John looked them all in the eye. "Hey, don't worry. Coach Phil is giving your parents a lecture about behaving and having fun on the other bus right about now too."

All the kids laughed and giggled, imagining their parents being told to behave themselves.

"All right, enjoy the rest of the trip. We have about another three or four hours until we arrive at the hotel." The kids all clapped and cheered,

and Coach John took a bow before settling into his seat and talking to some of the other adults that had ridden on the kids' bus with them.

"So, how's it going with you and Cam?" Violet asked Mia, leaning over the leather seat to try and talk to Mia two rows back. Violet played forward for the Hurricanes and was dating Linkin from the boys' team.

"Shh, he's just over there!" Mia said, shushing her friend as she blushed. Mia had joined the team at the start of the season and was currently dating Cameron, the captain of the boys' team.

"Please, half the bus heard that. For sure Cam did!" Linkin shot back at Mia, laughing hysterically. Linkin was usually one of the quieter members of the team, which was funny because he played defense for the Lightning, and his large size usually made people assume he'd be big and loud. He'd been coming out of his shell lately, however, and his signature black pants and red plaid shirt was never far away from any action.

"Enough, Link! Mia's already embarrassed enough without you making it worse. Sorry, Mia. Sometimes I don't realize how loud I'm talking. Forget the boys. Are we going to take home this trophy this year? I don't want a repeat of last year!"

"I'll second that!" Millie said. Last year at the same tournament, the Staten Saints had come out of nowhere to smash the Hurricanes in the final. They'd been up five goals, with only ten minutes left in the last period, when the Saints had not only leveled the scores but had gotten one up with only seconds left on the clock.

"I still can't believe that happened," Khloe said angrily. Even though it wasn't all her fault, as the goalie, she took a lot of the blame on her shoulders. Even the best goalie could only do so much without the support of her teammates, but that game had turned her from hero to zero in ten minutes flat, and it still stung.

"Shake it off, Khloe, that's not happening this year. We're going to be right beside you. Nothing is getting through," Millie said as she leaned over and hugged Khloe. No one blamed Khloe, but they all knew every goal that slid into the net was a personal defeat for the bubbly, quirky goalie.

"Has anyone stayed at this hotel before?" Logan asked loudly from the back seat, his question silencing the chatter on the bus almost instantly. Logan was the goalie for the Lightning and seemed to be continuing the strange tradition of goalies being just a little bit odd. Logan was also

Millie's cousin, which made him very protective of the Hurricane's captain. On and off the ice.

"Logan? Let's keep it down, buddy," Coach John said from the front of the bus, rubbing his forehead dramatically, not even bothering to turn and identify the loud culprit. You could guarantee if someone was loud, it was Logan. *It was going to be a long bus ride*, Coach John sighed with resignation.

"Sorry, coach!" Logan shouted back, barely stifling a laugh.

"Seriously dude, you're going to get us in trouble," Rhys muttered under his breath, "and that's my job!"

"You're just jealous someone's getting more attention than you, Rhys," Mia added, jumping to Logan's defense. Even though Mia had joined the girls' team at the start of the season, she had fit right in, soon becoming close friends with everyone and boys from both teams.

"You think we can clean sweep the away tournaments this year?" Cam asked the group of boys sitting around him.

"Taking Icefest would be a start. I've heard they have some of the best swag," Ben chimed in. Ben was one of their biggest and strongest defensive players, but he had an artistic side too. He loved to draw comics and had created some impressive hockey-related comics based on the two teams. He also had a massive crush on Lola, the Lightning's left wing.

Lola, too, loved to hang out with Ben and draw and was secretly crushing on him back, but so far, they had both been too shy to make the first move.

"What sort of swag?" Linkin asked.

"Well, I heard the winners all get the usual medals and a trophy, but they also give away a sweet Bauer hockey bag filled with stuff."

"That would be awesome!" Cam said joining in.

The rest of the long bus trip was relatively uneventful, with most of the kids talking and gossiping. A round of singing competitions had been quickly stopped by Coach John, who had announced the contestants on American Idol had nothing to fear from this group of kids and that he couldn't listen to their "screeching" another minute longer.

As the bus pulled up in front of the large hotel, the kids all scrambled to look out the windows.

"Look at the sign!" Mia shouted excitedly, pointing towards the front of the hotel.

"All right. Before you all run off, we need to check in. Now, it's already late, so no pool tonight. Just hang out in reception until all your parents are checked in, then head up to your rooms. We have a big day tomorrow, so plenty of rest—no mini sticks in the hallways, and no running around the place. I'll see you all bright and early for breakfast at 8 am. Have a good night's sleep!" Coach John finished speaking and stepped aside, barely avoiding being knocked over as all the kids rushed off the bus.

It was going to be a big day tomorrow, and the kids were full of energy now, but by this time tomorrow night, they'd be completely drained. It was a long weekend, and Coach John hoped they would be able to come away with the win by the end of the tournament.

2

"OMG! THEY HAVE a cook over there making omelets," Sage said as she slid into the booth next to Violet and Khloe.

"Trust you to be more interested in an omelet bar than the game coming up, Sage," Violet said, laughing.

"I can't help it that I'm going to be a chef and food interests me. Besides, we need our strength for the game this morning, and that stack of waffles and maple syrup is not going to help," Sage replied smugly, looking down her nose at what her teammates had on their plates.

"I have bacon," Khloe said between mouthfuls.

The rest of the girls all laughed hysterically until Lola ended up spitting her cereal all over the table, which only made the rest laugh harder.

"Enough, you lot. Now, finish your breakfast, grab your gear, and be at the bus in ten minutes. In case you forgot, we're here to play hockey," Coach Phil said from where he was sitting with some of the parents.

"Yes, coach!" The girls all shouted together.

"I haven't finished my bacon," Khloe said quietly to no one in particular. That set them all off laughing again until it spread around the entire breakfast room, and Coach Phil shrugged and gave up.

"Whoa, check out those kids in suits!" Cam said as he pointed to a team a little older than them walking across the parking lot.

"Those dudes are way serious," Hunter said, looking across to where the team in suits was entering the arena.

"Don't be intimidated by the suits and serious looks, guys. They're here to play, and we have just the same chance of winning as they do. Besides, you guys look pretty impressive in your track suits; that's why we wear them," Coach John said, standing up. "Now, grab your bags and wait next to the bus, and we'll walk into the arena as a team."

The two teams had traveled on different buses to the large arena. A few of the parents had come on the buses with the kids, but most of them had traveled separately because the coaches liked to talk to the kids on the way to and from the games.

"Each team is only playing one game today. Apparently, we have a pass this afternoon. Today's game is in Arena A for the Hurricanes and Arena D for the Lightning. Change room A-6 for the girls and D-9 for the boys. Both teams need to head up to the change room and get their warm-up gear on, and then we'll meet back here for a warm-up run together."

Both teams headed up through the crowded arena until they found their change rooms. There had to be over a thousand people crammed into the arena. Some teams were trying to warm up beside their change rooms while others were making their way out to play.

"This is crazy!" Millie shouted to the rest of the girls as they made their way into the change room.

"Has everyone got their jerseys?" Janet, the team manager, asked. Janet was the girls' team manager and took care of organizing which tournaments they entered and booking the hotels, team meals, and events. "I have spares, but I'll need to know sooner rather than later!"

Everyone had their jerseys for once, and the seriousness of the day started to set in as the girls quietly got into their warm-up gear.

Across the hall in the boys' change room, things weren't going as smoothly.

"What do you mean, you forgot your stick?" Coach John shouted at Rhys. "You're here to play hockey. Your hockey stick is one of the only things you need to do that!"

"Coach, I think it's just on the bus..." Rhys stuttered, looking somewhere slightly off to the left of the coach's angry red face.

"You think? Rhys, the day you start thinking is the day I start worrying. Now, for your sake, I suggest you run out to the carpark with your dad and find the bus. When you find the bus, you better hope for your sake there is one lonely stick on there. Then meet us for warm up. Are we clear?"

"Crystal clear, coach!" Rhys said hitting the door to the change room in a flash.

"Anyone else forgotten anything?" Coach John asked, glaring around the change room.

"Dude, I think I forgot my jock," Logan whispered to Cameron.

"Don't say anything. His vein might pop," Cam whispered back.

"We're good, and I found my jock!" Logan said holding up his jock. The rest of the boys burst into laughter as Coach John opened his mouth to say something and then thought better of it.

"We're comedians today, huh? That's good. Did I tell you the one about the hockey team that liked to make jokes?"

"No, coach. What about the hockey team that liked to make jokes?" Luke asked in all seriousness.

"Don't, Luke, it's—" Cam started to say before the coach interrupted him.

"Well, glad you asked, Luke. The team that liked to make jokes liked to run laps too. Lots of laps until they couldn't run anymore."

"Coach, that's not so funny," Hunter said shaking his head.

"Neither is forgetting stuff. Now, get your butts into gear and meet me at the warm-up area. The girls are probably waiting for us."

"I don't get it," Hunter whispered. The rest of the boys just groaned and finished getting ready.

Today was off to a bad start, and if they lost now, Coach John really would run them until they couldn't walk afterward.

3

AS THE TWO coaches had predicted, the first game for both teams were uneventful. The Hurricanes beat their opponents 4-1, while the Lightning won 3-0 with a shutout for Logan, the Lightning goalie. Khloe, the Hurricanes' goalie, wasn't as lucky. A puck clipped one of her own defender's skates and bounced into the net early in the last period.

After the two teams got changed, they headed out to the buses where the two coaches were waiting to have a chat with the players and parents.

"Okay everyone, great first game. We thought that one would be easy, but you all applied great pressure and played it like it was a final. Good commitment. Thanks to the parents for ensuring everyone showed up on time. Now what we really wanted to talk about was the special event we have planned for tonight. Coach Phil?"

"Yeah, like Coach John said, great first game. If we keep up that level of skill and pressure, it's going to be a great tournament. As for the special event, we're all going to an NHL game tonight! I've already spoken to everyone's parents, and everything is all organized. Make sure you thank Janet for organizing this surprise for us. So, we're going to have a team dinner before the hockey game then take the buses over there. And, as a bonus, the tournament organizers nabbed us some swag bags from the local team."

"That's awesome! Thanks, Janet!" Rhys shouted out. All the other kids either shouted their thanks too or nodded and agreed. Janet waved back, instantly turning a bright crimson and trying to hide from all the attention.

"Okay, before we head back to the hotel, I want to take a moment to remind you all that we have a game early tomorrow. Really early. 7:30 am. Bit of trade-off for the easy first day, I guess. There aren't any events scheduled today, so you can have some free time in the games room or the pool back at the hotel. We need everyone down at the buses, though, by 4:30 for dinner and the game," Coach John continued.

"Are there any events planned for tomorrow, coach?" Kiera, one of the juniors, asked.

"Well, they have a speed-skating competition that runs for the whole tournament that starts tomorrow. I also know for sure that there are shooting competitions for accuracy and hardest shot, and there's even a goalie competition."

"How do we enter?" Cameron asked.

"The heats are posted on the boards, and you just write your name next to a time slot to enter. If you make it through the heats, you'll compete in the semifinals and finals between games over the rest of the tournament."

Half the kids had already forgotten about the upcoming NHL game and were talking excitedly amongst themselves about the speed-skating and skills competitions.

"All right, before we all get carried away, don't forget to be on the bus at 4:30 tonight. Great first game everyone and let's head back to the hotel!"

The bus ride back to the hotel on that first day of the tournament wasn't spent talking about the NHL game, but which competitions everyone was going to enter the following day.

"I thought they'd be more excited about the NHL game," Coach John said to Coach Phil.

"They are, but we have two teams of seriously competitive kids here. They'll love the game but being the best shot or fastest skater is where it's at for them."

"I guess you're right. Either way, it looks like it's going to be an awesome tournament."

"Cannonball!" Hunter screamed as he came tearing into the pool area and threw himself into the deep end of the pool.

"Hunter! Come on, dude. You got my towel wet," Luke said from where he was sitting beside Cameron, Millie, and Mia.

"I'm not going to remind you again about the rules of the pool, mister!" Hunter's mom shouted from the deck chair she was relaxing in beside the pool as she tried to wipe pool water from her magazine.

"Sorry, Mom," Hunter replied sheepishly.

"Hunter got in trouble! Hunter got in trouble!" Daylyn teased, splashing water in Hunter's face.

"I don't think that's appropriate either, miss," Daylyn's dad said as he walked into the pool area. "You're not so old that I won't send you back to the room."

"Now look who's in trouble!" Hunter said, laughing as Daylyn turned crimson. Daylyn decided she'd pushed her luck far enough and bit her tongue, rolling her eyes at Hunter when her dad wasn't looking.

Someone threw some balls into the pool, and the kids quickly divided themselves into two teams and started playing dodgeball. If any of the other guests staying at the pool were interested in swimming, they soon decided against it once they saw the pack of hockey players laughing, squealing, and tearing around the pool area.

Millic decided she'd had enough of the dodgeball game, so she dragged herself out of the pool and spread her towel out on the grass.

"Hi!" said a tall, athletic-looking boy as he put his towel down beside hers on the grass.

"Umm, hey," Millie replied.

"Sorry, didn't mean to intrude. My name's Liam. I noticed you yesterday when you arrived at the tournament, but I didn't get a chance to say hello."

"Oh, cool. My name's Millie, but my friends all call me Mills. Who do you play for?"

"Nice to meet you, Mills. Umm, I'm the captain for the High Valley Blue Devils."

"Oh, cool. Have you guys played yet?"

"Yeah, we played yesterday and won. Coach reckons we've got a pretty good chance of winning the tournament. Actually, our biggest competition is going to be the Lightning."

"Nice. My best friend is the captain of the Lightning; he's over there in the pool playing dodgeball," Millie said, pointing out Cameron amongst the kids in the pool.

Just as Millie pointed Cameron out, he happened to look over to where Millie was lying in the grass talking to Liam.

"Hey, Linkin. Who's that talking to Mills?" Cameron asked, pausing in the middle of their game.

"Beats me, but I know the Blue Devils are staying in our hotel. Most likely, it's one of their players." Linkin was always the first to find out all the gossip about rival teams. He'd often sit and watch other teams practice at the tournaments.

"Man, what's she doing talking to the enemy? Those guys are our competition," Rhys said as he joined the two boys in looking to where Millie was sitting talking and laughing with Liam.

"I don't know. Forget about it for now; I'll talk to her after," Cameron said to the two boys. Both Linkin and Rhys could tell Cameron wasn't happy about the situation but weren't sure if it was because Millie was talking to the competition or because she was talking to another boy.

Cameron was currently dating Mia, but there had always something between Millie and Cameron. Everyone had been surprised when they hadn't ended up dating each other.

Just then, Janet, the team manager, walked into the pool area with her clipboard, and after a quick look around, headed to the pool.

"Hey y'all, there's only an hour until we need to leave for the hockey game tonight, so it's time to jump out of the pool and start getting ready. As it's a team event, we want everyone in their casual uniforms for tonight. If you need anything, let me know before we leave. I'll be in the common room on the second floor."

Janet's announcement led to a uniform sigh of discontent throughout the pool area, but the kids all grabbed their gear and headed up to the rooms.

"You think they'll have hot dogs at the game?" Violet asked Linkin as they headed to the elevators.

"Does a bear poop in the woods?" Linkin replied.

"What has that got to do with hot dogs?" Violet asked, shaking her head. Linkin didn't reply. He just rolled his eyes and laughed to himself as the elevator stopped.

"Seriously, you are a weirdo sometimes, Link. You're lucky I'm your girlfriend. I'm not sure anyone else could put up with you. Talking about hot dogs and bears in the woods. Weird."

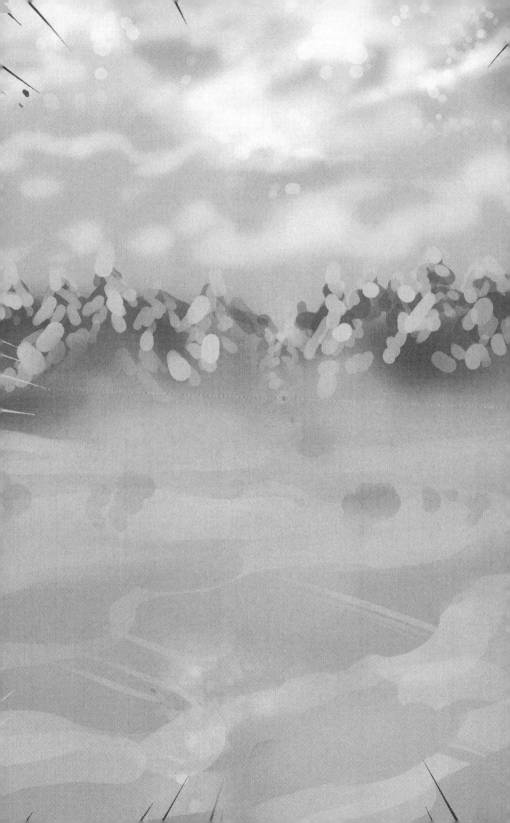

4

THE CARPARK OUTSIDE the arena was packed full of buses and cars all trying to park or drop people off. The atmosphere was electric as thousands of people dressed in their team's colors streamed through the large glass entrance and headed towards the ice.

"Okay, listen up and listen good, y'all. I'm only going to say this once!" Janet shouted from the front of the bus, her strong southern accent kicking up a notch. "We're seated in section 101A. I'm going to give y'all your tickets as you get off the bus. Once we get to the assigned seats you can swap around. If anyone gets lost at the arena, then head back to the security station at the entrance. I'll check in there every thirty minutes."

"I'd like to add something to what Janet has

said. You're all wearing our team uniforms. That means you're representing our team, our town, and each other. I know I don't need to tell you to be on your best behavior because you're all young adults now."

"Coach John is right. We know you'll do the right thing. Enjoy the game and have fun," Coach Phil added from his spot next to Coach John at the front of the bus.

The kids all cheered and clapped. They climbed off the bus, grabbed their tickets from Janet as they exited, and joined the crowd of people streaming into the arena.

"You think they'll be okay?" Janet asked the two coaches as they stood watching the kids line up in front of the entrance.

"For sure. They're a good bunch of kids. Except Rhys. I swear, that boy will be the death of me!" Coach John said rubbing his temple. "Anyway, let's get in there before we become the first coaches to lose thirty kids at a hockey game."

"These seats are amazing!" Violet shouted to the girls sitting around her.

"You're not wrong, Vi. I feel like I could almost

reach out and touch the players on the ice," Khloe added.

"Oh, and how cool is it when they get put in the penalty box? I still can't believe number 33 signed those autographs for us. His coach looked so mad!"

"I know, right? Like seriously mad. Imagine how mad Coach Phil would be if you tried pulling that stunt." All the girls giggled and glanced over to where their coach was sitting. When he looked over at them, it only made them giggle and laugh even more.

"What do you think they're all laughing at?" Coach Phil asked Janet, frowning.

"Stop frowning and worrying, Phil. They're probably laughing about something silly, not you. Y'all and Coach John need to learn how to relax!"

"Well, they're looking right at us, and now they're laughing even harder!"

"Coach Phil and Janet are staring right at us! Stop looking at them and laughing. They'll think we're up to something," Millie hissed at the other girls before bursting into laughter herself.

Right then the home team pushed forward and scored a goal. The arena burst into cheers and the boys all stood on their seats and started cheering.

This earned them a few cheers from some serious fans sitting behind them who threw the boys some team flags and a cowbell.

Rhys grabbed that cowbell and shook it like crazy, which only stirred up even more enthusiasm in the kids.

"This cowbell is the best thing ever!" Rhys screamed as he shook it back and forth every time the home team took possession of the puck.

As the siren sounded to signal the end of the first period, the score was 1-0, with neither team able to penetrate the other's defense much beyond that one goal. Both goalies were working overtime, however, with plenty of shots heading their way, but none of them found their way into the back of the net.

The intermission between the first and second period was the perfect opportunity for the kids to hit the concession stands and the toilets. When they all piled back into their seats, their arms were full of pop, hot dogs, popcorn, and nachos.

"I love hockey hot dogs the best!" Cameron said, leaning over to where his girlfriend Mia was sitting next to his best friend, Millie.

"You love any hot dogs!" Millie shouted back

over the roar of the crowd as the two teams skated back out onto the ice.

"I've never seen him turn down any junk food," Mia added to Millie.

"I know, right? He eats like the main food groups are fast food, sugar, grease, and fat. You better watch out if he ever quits hockey or gets injured. He'll balloon!" Millie imitated a big balloon with her arms and laughed.

"Hey, how about we stop worrying about what I eat and focus on the game?" Cameron added, not exactly enjoying this sort of attention.

"Hey, Mills, isn't that your boyfriend sitting in the section across from us?" Khloe asked sweetly, with a big smirk on her face.

Millie looked across to where Khloe was pointing and saw Liam, the captain of the High Valley Blue Devils, looking back at her and smiling. Millie couldn't help but instantly blush a deep red at having been caught looking at him.

"Khloe! You made it look like we were all staring at him!" Millie said, throwing a handful of popcorn at Khloe. Khloe jumped up in her seat trying to catch some in her mouth, but unfortunately most of it ended up landing on Coach Phil and Janet.

"Seriously? Who's throwing popcorn?!" Coach Phil shouted.

"Y'all better behave yourselves, otherwise you're going to be sitting right next to me where I can keep an eye on you," Janet said.

A round of "Sorry," and "It won't happen again," quickly came from Millie and the other kids. Millie looked over to where Liam was sitting with the rest of his team and thought about how cute he looked dressed up. Just then, he looked up again, and this time it was Millie who caught him checking her out. They both blushed and managed a little wave before Liam turned back to watch the game with the rest of his friends.

"Hey, do you think Coach Phil and Janet would make a cute couple?" Sage asked, leaning over the back of Millie's and Mia's seats.

"For sure. We should set them up or something," Khloe replied, just as a big squirt of ketchup and mustard shot out of her hot dog and all over her jersey.

"Duh. Now I gotta go and try and clean this off. My parents will kill me," she said as she unsuccessfully tried to wipe off the messy sauces with a paper napkin.

"I'll go with you," Mia added as she stood up out of her seat.

Just then, the home team finally managed to get through the visitor's defense and score a goal. The whole arena erupted with cheers, screaming, shouts, and Rhys's cowbell. One of the guys seated behind them jumped up and bumped into Mia, who went sprawling into Cameron's lap.

"Sorry!" the guy shouted to Mia, reaching out to offer his hand to help her back up. "Got a little bit too excited there. Did you spill your drink? Jeez, I'm sorry."

"It's okay," Mia replied as Cameron and Millie helped her up.

"Nope. It's not. Look, here's some money to buy another pop and some snacks for you and your friend."

"Thanks. You ready Khloe?"

"Yep. Let's go," Khloe replied as the two girls pushed their way through the cheering crowd and headed to the washroom to get cleaned up.

No one else scored for the remainder of the game, so the home team took the win and the crowd cheered them on the whole way. At the end of the game, the Hurricanes and Lightning moved down closer to the tunnel where the players were lined up and signing autographs. They had to wait almost fifteen minutes to get their autographs, but it was well worth it because then all the kids had jerseys signed by the team.

As the kids all piled onto their buses for the trip back to the hotel, one small group at the back of the bus was quietly plotting how they could get Coach Phil and Janet together.

5

"YOUR MOM IS so funny, Daylyn," Sage said as the pair of girls grabbed their hockey bags from the bus's luggage compartment.

The girls' team was half asleep as they dragged their equipment off the bus and headed to the large arena doors.

"Thanks. She loves helping out as the team manager. Plus, it means I find out all the gossip before everyone else."

"Haha, true! Jeez, I hate these early morning games. I swear, I would trade my left arm for two or three more hours of sleep," Sage replied sleepily, rubbing her eyes and yawning dramatically.

"Coach? Coach!" Khloe shouted as she tried to pull her oversized goalie bag from the bus's luggage area unsuccessfully.

"You need a hand, Khloe?" Coach Phil shouted as he started heading over to give his goalie a hand.

"Yes, please. And how many games have we got today? I could use a little more beauty sleep."

"Khloe, you look amazing. You always do!" Millie said as she walked past, rolling her hockey bag.

"Why thank you, Mills," Khloe said as she curtsied dramatically like a princess, "but we all know that this," Khloe said gesturing toward her face, "doesn't happen all by itself." The rest of the girls all laughed as they watched Coach Phil and Khloe drag her large bag out.

When they finally yanked the bag out, Coach Phil straightened with a wince and launched into his spiel. "We have the 8:30 am. game first and then another at 12:30 pm. There are two pools of four teams in our age group. The top two teams from each pool will play off tonight in the semifinal games. The winners of those two games will play off tomorrow for gold and silver, while the losers will play off for bronze and fourth place. If we finish first in our pool, we'll play second in the other pool."

"So, we need to win both games this morning

to have the best chance of finishing in first right, coach?" Daylyn asked.

"Yes, Daylyn, it's always best to finish on top of your pool in tournaments because it gives you the easiest track to the finals. Anyway, enough chit chat. Let's get into the arena and get into our warm-up suits. I'll meet you girls next door at the indoor track in the same place as yesterday."

The girls all nodded and streamed into the arena. There were a lot of kids and parents already at the arena, even though it was only 7:00 am. Normally, the coach would expect them all to be there earlier than they were, but the arena only opened the main doors at 6:30 am.

As the girls all walked into the change room to get their equipment ready, Janet walked in with a large cardboard box.

"What's in the box?" Mia asked Millie, leaning over to try and look into the large box.

"Beats me," Millie replied, who was just as curious as her friend.

"It's your swag bags, y'all. I'll put one on top of each of your bags while you're playing so you can grab them straight after," Janet replied, pushing the box into the corner out of the way. "Coach Phil doesn't want me to give them out before the game, so y'all will just have to hold your horses."

"I wonder what we get?" Emma asked one of the other juniors, Kiera, who just shrugged as she stood up and pushed her bag under the bench.

The rest of the girls were doing the same, hanging their jerseys on the hooks behind the bench and laying out some of their equipment ready for after their warm-up. They wouldn't have a lot of time to get into their skates and other equipment, so it was easier to get organized now.

The boys were still back at the hotel just getting up for breakfast. They didn't have to play until 10:30 am., but their coach had asked if they wanted to go and watch the girls play and cheer them on.

"Seriously, I think I could handle having a buffet-breakfast-type setup at my house. You think my mom would go for it?' Logan asked as he piled another plate full of waffles and bacon.

"Dude, I think if you had a buffet breakfast at your house, you'd end up being bigger than a house judging by the amount of bacon and waffles your putting away," Rhys piped up from the other side of the table, winking at their goalie.

"Hey! I'm a growing boy. You think it's easy stopping all those shots from the other teams that you guys just let walk in?" Logan shot straight back.

"Please, half the game you're just sitting down cleaning your crease and waving at people," Ben chimed in, nudging his defense partner, Linkin. Both boys burst into laughter, with Linkin spraying chewed-up fruit salad all over his plate.

"Enough! Remember, we're all a team here. We play better when we all work as one. Save the banter for when you're on the ice," Coach John said as he slid his finished plate to one side.

Coach John had been one of the best hockey players in their league, having played professionally for a national hockey team for over six years. After he had retired from professional hockey, he'd started his own coaching business, and now he coached their team as a favor to one of the player's dads. He didn't have any of his own kids, so he enjoyed mentoring the boys, and never complained about the time and effort he gave to the team.

"Well?" Coach John asked. "Are we all ready to go? The bus leaves in five minutes, so if you miss it, you'll need to get a ride with your parents. See you downstairs, and Rhys?"

"Yes, coach?" Rhys asked quietly for once.

"Don't forget anything. Okay? Or I'll forget to play you, and you'll be sitting on the bench handing out water bottles the entire game. Are we clear, buddy?"

"Crystal clear, coach," Rhys replied sheepishly.

The other boys all laughed and giggled. It was always funny when someone else was getting unwanted attention from the coach.

"Quit it, you guys," Rhys said unhappily as he pushed his plate to one side. He wasn't going to waste any of his five minutes and headed up to his room to double-check his hockey bag for the third time that morning.

It was the start of the third period, and the girls were down by one goal. So far, it had been a low scoring but fiercely competitive game, with the scores sitting at 3-2 and both teams failing to convert their advantages.

The Hurricanes were starting to feel the pressure of performing in front of large crowds as the arena was packed full of teams and people cheering. All the parents were in their team clothes as the visitor's section of the stands was packed full of Dakota Hurricanes team wear. Some of the younger siblings had been busy too. They were pressed up against the glass in the Hurricanes' end of the ice with a large banner they had made back at the hotel the night before.

As the referee blew the whistle to start the final period, the girls refocused and prepared for one final push to try and take back the game.

The first half of the final period followed the rest of the game, with neither team being able to punch through the defense and score. There had been opportunities to score for both teams, but both goalies were on fire, with neither team being able to convert.

Now they were down to less than four minutes of play.

"We need to break this up!" Millie shouted as she skated through the open gate and threw herself down on the bench.

"I know, right? That goalie is as tough as Khloe," Mia panted from beside Millie.

"I need both of you to push harder. They're getting tired and have started to shorten their defensive shifts, but now I need you both to take a double shift. I'm going to wait to let you out until their third defense line goes out," Coach Phil said from where he was standing behind them.

"Is that their weakest line? The one with 66 and 23 in it?" Mia asked.

"Yep, it's also their most tired. They're slow to react now, so I'm going to pressure them with you two. Now, get ready because in thirty seconds you're going out again."

Mia and Millie shuffled down the bench until they sat at the gate, ready to go out. Both of them were intently watching the game and the other team's bench out of the corner of their eyes.

"Okay, when they change, you're changing. Just be ready to go when I shout."

Mia and Millie knew what they had to do and didn't need to be told twice. They both stood, ready to go, Mia taking a final drink of water and adjusting the chin strap on her helmet out of habit.

"Change, change, change!" Coach Phil screamed. Like most coaches, he wasn't afraid to give it 110% when it came to screaming as loudly as he could.

Mia and Millie hit the ice within a second of each other and just as Sage passed the puck over before hitting the bench.

Mia and Millie moved the puck forward together, acting like they had the whole game whenever they were moving forward and setting up a play, but this time was different. They didn't wait for the rest of the team to complete the change, catching the other team off guard.

Millie flicked the puck to Mia as they skated past the last defender, who was desperately skating backward, trying to ward off the two forwards. Just as Mia thought she was past the defender, her skates hit the other girl's stick, and she felt herself losing control. At the last second, she flicked the puck back to Millie before falling in a tangled heap with the defender.

It was all up to Millie now as she skated full speed at their goalie. The goalie matched each move Millie made. When she faked to the left, the goalie didn't flinch, and now, Millie was committed to the angle. Millie pulled her stick back and sent the puck flying toward the top corner of the net, right over the goalie's shoulder.

The goalie tried desperately to stop the shot, but the puck was too fast...

The Hurricanes were already standing, but their cheering was a little too eager as the puck touched the crossbar and sailed off into the net.

As the clock continued to count down, Millie skated back to where Mia was picking herself up off the ice.

"So close! Good try, Mills," Mia said as the pair headed to where the referee was waiting to set off a faceoff.

"Not good enough. We're down to a minute left, and we're a goal down," Mille replied. It didn't look good for the Hurricanes.

The rest of the game, what was left of it, was anticlimactic as the opposition burned the clock down until the final siren sounded.

The Hurricanes had lost their second game 3-2. The girls skated off the ice and headed quietly into the change room.

"Sorry, guys, I let you down," Khloe said quietly.

"Don't say that, Khloe. You had an amazing game. If it weren't for you, the score would have been even bigger. They just had a great defense, and their goalie was on fire today. We can't win them all. We can just play the best we can, and we all did that today," Millie said.

"Mills is right. All you girls had an amazing first game this morning, and I'm proud of you. Now, grab your gear and get changed. Remember to grab your swag bags, and then go rest up for your 12:30 game. You only have a couple hours, so make sure you eat and drink. No fries and junk food. I'll see you at 11:30 for game two. And the boys were nice enough to get up early and watch your game, so make sure you don't miss theirs at 10:30," Coach Phil said as he left the change room so the girls could change.

"He's right, you know. We're not out of this tournament yet. Now, who's going to win the next game?!" Violet shouted.

"We are!" the girls shouted back.

"I can't hear you!" Violet shouted. "Who's going to win?"

"Hurricanes! Hurricanes! Hurricanes!" The girls all screamed together.

6

THE GIRLS HAD had a tough game two, but now it was time for the boys to see if they could come out on top in their second game of the tournament. If only Cam could concentrate on the hockey instead of that guy Millie was talking with.

"Who are we playing?" Rhys asked Cameron, trying to snap his friend out of the distracted mood that he was in as they walked over to the other pad.

"Umm, I think an easier team this morning. Coach John said they were ranked a lot further down than us in the state."

"If they're ranked so low, how did they make it into an A tournament?" Rhys asked. "I mean, I know why we're here, but we ranked high. We always do."

"They were high last year, but this year they aren't doing as well, I guess. Like us, they would have booked all their tournaments long before this year's team was even assembled."

"That makes sense. Or maybe it's because their team isn't as balanced with juniors and seniors like ours. That means they'd have a weaker team every other year."

"True. That could be it too," Cameron replied.

"Hey, if we win these two games today, we play tonight in the semis, right?' Ben asked, catching up with the two boys.

"Yep. We win these, it's semifinals tonight. It's going to be at a sucky time, though. Semifinals for our group are scheduled for 6:30 pm."

"I wonder if we'll get pizza? It'll be too late to go out anywhere, and most of the parents will just want to hang out and gossip anyway," Rhys added.

"Seriously, Rhys? Try to think of something other than your stomach. Just. For. Once," Ben added. Of all their teammates, if anyone was going to bring up food, it was going to be Rhys. Last year they'd had a hot-dog day to help raise money for the club, and Rhys was currently the club's hot-dog eating champion.

"How many hot dogs did you eat that day last year?" Cameron asked his friend.

"22," Rhys said flatly. "It'll be 30 this year if we can get my mom to mind her own business," Rhys added with a scowl.

"Dude, you were going to throw up," Cameron said poking Rhys in the stomach.

"No way!" Rhys was still annoyed his mom had shown up and dragged him off the stage right as he'd been going for his twenty-third hot dog. "I'm going to set a hot-dog eating record no one will beat."

"Don't count on it, buddy. I heard that new goalie has been practising, and judging by the look of him, he can go the distance," Ben added puffing himself up to look bigger.

"Please. He's got nothing on this eating—"

"What Rhys? Who's got nothing on eating what?" Coach John asked as the trio walked into the change room.

"Ah, umm. Nothing, coach, just talking about hot dogs," Rhys answered quickly as his two friends started laughing.

"Well gentlemen, how about we get our butts into our gear and get ready to go for a warm-up run? The rest of the team is patiently waiting. There's a time to talk about hot dogs, and it isn't now!"

As expected, the boys didn't mess around when they hit the ice and carved up the opposition team to advance to the first final. With the girls cheering them on from the glass, they rose to the occasion and set a hard pace early and got off to a 3-0 lead after the first period.

They didn't let off the gas when they came out after the first-period break, and they piled on another two goals to take their lead to 5-0.

The other team wasn't terrible, but the Lightning boys weren't giving them any opportunities. A strong defense combined with Logan's top-notch goaltending meant there were limited opportunities for the other team to try and claw their way back into the game.

After they hit the ice for the last period, the coaches took the opportunity to start trying some different line combinations and advanced plays the boys had been practising.

When the final siren sounded at the end of the game, they had taken their lead from five goals to eight goals, and Logan had earned a shutout. No goals had been scored on him, and the giant pile on at the end of the game was the closest he'd ever been crushed alive.

The other team was noticeably disappointed, and the Lightning boys went out of their way to make sure they thanked not only the refs but also their opposition and the coaches. They skated off the ice with their heads held high and a standing ovation from the girls' team, who were banging on the glass.

The girls' second game of the day went much better, and they took an easy 4-1 win, coming second in their pool overall. They would be playing the first-place team in group B, which was one of the strongest teams in the state. This team had more seniors than the Hurricanes, which meant they had bigger players. The Hurricanes would need to play faster and smarter if they were to stand a chance of beating their rivals.

7

THE BOYS TOOK another win for their third game of the tournament, but it wasn't a cake walk like their first game of the day, which they had won easily. Their opposing team now wasn't pulling any punches when it came to the physical side of the game.

It was late in the third period and the boys were up 3-2 over the other team. A late hit on Linkin took him down on the ice hard, and he wasn't getting up. Coach John and the trainer walked out onto the ice as the other players all took a knee.

After a few tense moments, Coach John and Tyler, the Lightning trainer, helped Linkin to his feet. They assisted him to the gate at the side of the arena where they were met by one of the tournament medics. The boys and crowd all cheered as Linkin slowly made his way off the ice.

"Dude, they're taking him off the ice!" Rhys yelled as he skated up beside Cameron. "That's not good; otherwise, they'd just keep him on the bench. Number four is mine!" Rhys spat out angrily as he started skating towards where the other team were gathered together.

"Rhys! Forget it! It's not worth it!" Cameron shouted as he tried to head Rhys off before he did anything stupid. "Damn it! Someone help me stop him!" Cameron shouted, trying to catch Rhys before he got himself thrown into the penalty box, or worse, kicked out of the game.

Cameron and Ben managed to stop Rhys before he did something stupid and steered him toward their bench just as Coach John walked back into the bench area.

"Linkin won't be back on the ice. He's going to be okay, but he landed badly on his shoulder and arm. Don't let this affect how you're playing. There's only five minutes left. Just stay the course and win this game for Linkin. Now, get back out there and don't let them in! This is our game. Win it for your teammate!"

They boys took Coach John's advice and won

the game. Despite winning though, the boys were subdued after their game. They were more worried about their teammate and what had happened to him. The door banged open and their team trainer, Tyler, walked in with their first-aid kit.

"How is Linkin?" Coach John asked before the boys all had a chance to jump in.

"Suspected broken arm. His parents and the first-aid staff took him to the local emergency room for an x-ray to confirm it, but I'd say he's fractured or broken it for sure," Tyler said before turning to the rest of the boys. "Look, guys, Linkin is okay. He's upset at letting you guys down, but he's doing okay. As soon as they know more, his parents will let me know and I'll let all of you know."

"Cameron, why don't you talk to the boys while Tyler and I talk outside? I'll give you five, ten minutes before I open the door to your parents."

"Thanks, coach." Cameron waited until the door had closed behind Coach John and Tyler before turning to his teammates. "Look, guys, I know it sucks what happened to Linkin, but we need to pull together now more than ever. We're going to win this tournament, and we're going to win it for Linkin! Okay?"

"For Linkin!" Rhys shouted.

"For who? I can't hear you!" Cameron shouted back.

"For Linkin!" The whole team shouted back.

"That's better! Now, let's get changed and get out of here. We've got another game tonight, and we need to be focused," Cameron said as the boys all gathered around, cheering. What had happened to Linkin was rotten, but it could be just the motivation the Lightening needed to push them over the finish line as they headed into the semifinals.

The girls were resting back at the hotel, eating lunch in the main dining area, when Coach Phil walked in and called them all to attention.

"Girls! Look, sorry to interrupt your lunch, but I have some bad news. Coach John just called me, and he told me Linkin was hit pretty bad toward the end of their last game."

"Oh, my God. Is he okay?!" Violet shouted as she jumped to her feet, knocking her lunch over in the process and spilling soup all over the table.

"He's been taken to the hospital, Violet. He walked off the ice, but they think he's broken his arm. He was hit late in the third period and fell badly. We'll know more once Linkin's parents let us know how the x-rays go."

All the girls huddled around Violet to comfort her when she started to cry.

"Violet, he's going to be okay," Coach Phil said softly to Violet as she sobbed on Millie's shoulder. The girls broke into small groups, their lunch largely forgotten as they talked about Linkin.

Mia and Millie guided Violet out of the dining area out toward the pool area where they could sit quietly and talk.

Fifteen minutes later, Coach Phil walked back downstairs and called all the girls together again, just as the boys were walking into the foyer.

"Okay, everyone. Boys, you might as well gather around too. Linkin's parents just called and the x-ray has confirmed his arm is broken." All the girls and boys were visibly shaken up. This was the first serious injury either of the two teams had ever had to deal with.

"Before everyone freaks out, Linkin is fine and told his dad to pass on that he wanted someone to save him some pie from lunch." This got some nervous laughter from the kids gathered around him. "He's going to be back at the hotel in about an hour or so. Now, we all have another game tonight, so make sure you all have your heads on straight and your gear ready."

Forty-five minutes later, everyone was sitting around the foyer with their hockey bags ready to head back to the arena. Tournaments were a lot of fun, but it didn't always leave as much time to relax and have fun between games as you might think.

The girls were trying to delay leaving as late as possible so Violet could get a chance to see Linkin when he got back from the hospital.

Just as they'd given up hope, Linkin's cab pulled into the main drop off outside the revolving door.

"Linkin!" Violet shouted as she dropped her bag and rushed toward Linkin as he slowly climbed out of the cab. "Jeez! Your arm is in a cast! Are you okay? Are you in pain?" All the questions Violet had been waiting to ask just burst out in a mad rush of gibberish.

"Vi, it's okay. My arm is broken, but I'll survive. Thank you for waiting, but your bus is waiting in the carpark. Good luck with your game. I'll be here when you get back, okay?" Linkin reached out and gently took Violet's hand and gave it a small squeeze. Now she knew he was okay and could concentrate on the upcoming game.

"Link! What's the verdict? You going to be

playing in the rest of the tournament?" Cameron asked as the rest of the boys and girls all gathered around.

"Hey everyone, thanks for waiting to see how I was. Umm, no I won't be playing in the rest of the tournament. The doctor told me I'd be lucky to play again this season. My arm is going to be in a cast for at least six to eight weeks."

This news was met by a loud chorus of groans and "that sucks" from the boys and girls surrounding him.

"I know, just bad luck really. Sorry, guys, I know you'll be down a player now," Linkin said, sheepishly looking down at his feet.

"Look, buddy, you weren't that good anyway. We'll hardly miss you!" Rhys said, slapping Linkin on his sore arm.

"Ow! Dude! My arm is broken! Geez," Linkin said, wincing. Rhys look mortified, but the slip up broke the tension and everyone laughed.

"Okay, welcome back, Linkin, but girls, the bus is leaving, and we need to be on it," Coach John said as he started herding the girls out of the hotel and toward the bus.

Violet turned and waved to Linkin as the boys all gathered around to start signing his cast.

Cameron looked and saw Millie waving at him, and he waved back before he realized she was looking past him. Cameron turned slowly to follow her gaze and saw she was actually waving at that Liam kid from the other team.

The team they still had to play. Cameron forgot what had happened to Linkin. He had something else to focus on now, and he didn't get why this was bothering him so much.

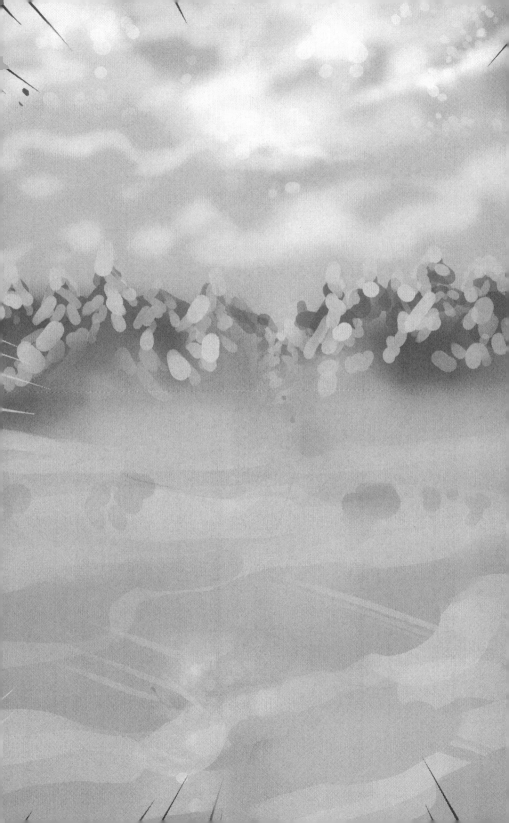

8

THE GIRLS ALL rolled into the arena, pumped and excited for their semifinal game against the Halton Dragons. The Hurricane girls didn't mess around in the change room and headed straight for the warm-up area.

The Halton Dragons were already there, warming up on the far side. Even from this distance, the girls could tell the team they were playing looked daunting.

"Whoa! They're huge!" Daylyn blurted out. Millie knew if they focused too much on the size of the other team, doubts would start to creep in before they'd even started playing. Luckily, she had an idea about how she could fix it.

"Daylyn? Can we use your mom's speaker?" Millie asked.

"Umm, sure. She put it in the change room. I'll just go grab it," Daylyn replied, jogging out of the warm-up area and back into the change room. Millie walked over to the bench and took her phone out of the gear bag, scrolling through her playlists.

"Bit late for texting isn't it, Millie?" Coach Phil said as he and Janet walked over to where Millie was standing with her phone.

"No, coach, I'm just going to try and get the girls pumped up for the game. Daylyn's gone to get your speaker from the change room, Janet. I hope that's okay?"

"Y'all can blast your music as loud as you like if it pumps you up. This ain't my first rodeo," Janet said with a wink. The girls set up the speaker and started blasting the team's favorite warm-up track as they warmed up.

"I don't know what they see in this music," Janet said to Coach Phil, shaking her head. "Give me some Garth Brooks any day of the week."

"You're a country fan? I love Garth Brooks!" Coach Phil said as he and Janet moved to the side.

"Maybe you didn't just fall off the turnip truck after all, Phil. There could be hope for you yet buster," Janet said with a wink, which caused Coach Phil to blush bright red.

"Look! They're hitting it off!" Sage said to Millie.

"Who is?" Daylyn asked, looking around before spotting her mom and her coach laughing together. "Oh, gross, guys. No way!" she blurted out.

"Can't stop true love, Daylyn!" Mia shouted as all the girls continued warming up, laughing as they did so. The other team's size was forgotten.

As the girls lined up on the ice to shake hands with the other team, the size difference truly was amazing.

"What the heck are they feeding them in Halton? It's like we're playing giants! Khloe said, eyeing up the other team, especially their goalie.

After they shook hands, Millie faced off against the opposition captain, who was stockier and at least a head taller.

The ref blew the whistle, and the Dragons won the faceoff, quickly moving the puck away from Millie. Violet moved to intercept but found herself in a 2 versus 1 against two much larger girls, who quickly pushed her off her line. They zipped around her for a quick pass and one timer, netting a goal in the top left corner.

It all happened so quickly Khloe was left

standing there looking shocked and shaking her head. This couldn't be happening.

As Millie and her line hit the bench for a change, she heard one of the juniors say, "This isn't going to end well."

"It's only one goal, and there's a whole lot of this game left. So, get on with it. They may be bigger than we are, but we're smarter, faster, and better. Don't forget that! If we let them control this game, then they're going to take it away from us. Remember who we are!"

Coach Phil nodded at Millie and from then on, it was game on.

The girls hadn't quite seized the momentum by the end of the first period, but they had managed to score one goal and limit the Dragons to only one other goal. It was 2-1 heading into the start of the second period.

It turned into a grind in the second period with the Hurricanes getting a breakaway in the dying minutes of the period to even the score. The Hurricanes' stamina and fitness was starting to show as they pushed the bigger team to the edge of their limits.

The girls hit the huddle as the siren sounded at the end of the second period.

"Great job, girls! They're making shorter and shorter shift changes and they are getting messy. It's time to kick it up a gear and break them. We've tied it up, and now we're going to show everyone why we deserve to win this! Don't get sucked into those physical battles near the net. They're stronger, but you're better. Outskate them. Just keep moving your feet. Remember, smarter not harder. Now, go get 'em!"

The scores were still tied ten minutes into the final period despite the best efforts of both teams' forwards. Khloe and the other goalie were on fire in their nets, not letting anything through.

With only a few minutes left, Daylyn took the puck from behind Khloe's net and darted toward the other end. The Hurricanes were doing a quick change, so Daylyn was desperately looking for an outlet as she pushed up the ice. She may not be the biggest or fastest, but she sure could move when she needed too!

As Daylyn crossed the other team's blue line, she saw Sage and Mia powering toward her from their bench. Daylyn headed around the boards and behind the other team's net, hugging them tight. The Dragons were desperate to get the puck from her, but this late in the game they couldn't risk earning a penalty. Just as Daylyn was about to head out from the net, the defense reached out for the puck but hooked her leg instead, pulling it out from under her and sending her crashing onto the ice, but not before she had managed to flick the puck toward the net.

Sage, struggling with the Dragons' defense in front of the net, managed to break free and get to the puck, barely, and tipped it toward the net. The goalie threw herself to the side, but the puck slid past and found the back of the net.

Goal! The entire arena erupted! The girls piled on Sage and Daylyn as the two made their way back to the bench. Then the new Hurricanes' line took the ice with less than sixty seconds left on the clock.

Despite everything the other team threw at them, the Hurricanes managed to hold out for the win. They made it to the championship game!

The boys had a much easier game in their semifinal. They took a 4-1 win over their opposing team and would be playing the Blue Devils in the championship game tomorrow. The problem was, the Blue Devils had also won all their games in their pool and were looking at a clean sweep if they beat the Lightning tomorrow.

9

"PIZZA PARTY!" RHYS shouted as he ran through the lobby of the hotel at full speed toward the pool area.

"Rhys! Stop screaming and running, or it'll be your last pizza party!" his dad shouted from the lobby area. The other boys all laughed and ran screaming after their friend. No one wanted to be the last one to the pool because not only would it close in an hour, but they knew their curfew was an early one tonight.

The boys and girls both made the most of the pool and made the normally quiet pool area of the hotel sound like an amusement park on a hot summer's day.

The parents organized enough pizzas to feed a small army and set up their coolers ready to enjoy the rest of the night once the kids were banished to their respective bedrooms. The boys and girls didn't mess around once the pizzas arrived, and there was soon a pile of empty pizza boxes littering the communal tables set up around the pool. The best part of the hotel was it had an arcade right there and lots of tables to sit around.

Millie decided to sneak out to grab some snacks from her room, and as she went to press the elevator button, the elevator door opened. Liam was standing there smiling at her.

"Going up?" he said with a large smile.

"Yes, thanks," Millie replied, pushing the button for the floor she was staying on.

Millie and Liam spent their time riding up in the elevator talking about how their games had gone that day. Liam told Millie they'd won their semis and now they would be playing the Lightning tomorrow.

"Oh, wow! Awesome!" Millie said smiling on the outside but already dreading how Cameron and the other boys would feel about it. She really liked Liam, but how could she support anyone other than her boys?

Millie and Liam were still chatting and laughing when the elevator door opened on Millie's floor.

Millie glanced out to see Cameron standing there. His large smile quickly faded away to be replaced by a dirty glare.

"Oh, hey, Cam," Millie said, blushing like she'd been caught doing something wrong. *This sucked so bad*, Millie thought. It wasn't fair that Cam was making her feel so bad about Liam. He had Mia, so why couldn't she have someone special?

"I have to go anyway, Millie. Coach set an early curfew. I'll see you tomorrow!" Liam said as he stepped past Cameron and gave Millie a wave.

"Night, Liam. Good luck tomorrow!" Millie replied, waving back to Liam as he headed down the hallway toward his room.

Cameron's anger was boiling up inside him while Liam and Millie said their goodbyes, and he was only seconds away from bursting.

"Seriously, Millie! What's up with you and that guy? You know he plays for the team we need to beat tomorrow! Whose side are you on anyway?" Cam blurted out, gesturing wildly as his voice got louder and louder in the narrow hallway.

"Don't even start with me, Cam! You're not my brother and you're not my boyfriend. I can talk to and hang out with whomever I like. In case you forgot, you already have a girlfriend." Millie stormed off down the hallway to get the snack she had originally gone up to get in the first place, leaving Cam to ride down in the elevator alone.

Cam walked back into the arcade room and sat by himself. Damn it. Why was he letting this Liam and Millie thing affect him so much? He was being an idiot, but he just couldn't stop himself.

"Dude, what's up with you? You look like someone just stole your bike," Luke said as he sat down beside his captain.

"Yeah, bro. You went upstairs fine and came back downstairs grumpy," Hunter chimed in. Just then, Millie walked back into the room, completely ignoring the three boys, and headed over to the other girls.

The two boys looked at Millie sitting with the girls, then looked at Cam and back at each other. Hunter rolled his eyes and Luke nodded. It didn't take a rocket scientist to figure out Cameron and Millie were seriously annoyed with each other.

This wasn't going to end well for either team. They had important games coming up tomorrow, and with their captains fighting, it could have disastrous results the next day. Just as Luke and Hunter were trying to wrap their heads around what could have gone wrong, Coach John and Coach Phil walked over the arcade area.

"Okay, boys and girls. This area is closing and it's almost curfew time. You can all have another hour, but you need to be in your rooms. Get a good night's sleep, and we'll see you bright eyed and bushy tailed in the morning!"

All the girls packed up and headed upstairs to Millie's room while the boys did the same but headed for Cameron's room.

Mia found herself sharing an elevator with Cameron, and she hadn't missed his foul mood.

"Cam, what's up with you? You're okay one minute, grouchy the next. Have I done something wrong?" Mia asked quietly as the elevator doors closed.

"No, Mia, you haven't done anything. It's Millie and that Liam guy. How come she thinks it's cool to hang out with the enemy?"

"Cam, I don't think he's your enemy. Liam is just another boy that loves hockey as much as you do. He just plays for another team. Millie would never do anything to hurt you or your team. Whether she has a crush on Liam or not, she'll be right there with us cheering you on tomorrow."

"I don't know, Mia. It just bugs me." Cam said feeling a little guilty about how he'd been behaving.

"Listen, do me a favor please. Message Millie before bed and tell her how you're feeling. It's not going to do any of us any good if you're both fighting and angry at each other."

"You're right. I'll text her. Anyway, I better get in my room before the coaches come and check. Night, Mia, and thanks for talking to me. It's helped a lot," Cam said hugging Mia.

"You're welcome, silly. Goodnight," Mia said, quickly hugging Cam back and then heading toward her room at the other end of the hallway.

Mia walked into Millie's room just as Georgia was asking Millie a question.

"So, Mills, what's up with you and that hottie from the other team?" Millie couldn't help but blush.

"Nothing!" Millie blurted out a little defensively.

"Millie has a crush! Millie has a boyfriend!" The girls chanted and laughed, throwing pillows and blankets at their friend.

"Sure, you're crushing on him hard, girl," Khloe added, poking Millie in the ribs. "Apart from that, anyone know what's up with Cam? He looks grumpy tonight! Mia?"

"Umm, I think he's just worried about being a player down tomorrow with Lincoln out," Mia replied, hesitating a bit, not wanting to come between Cameron and Millie.

"It's because I was talking to Liam in the elevator, and Cameron saw us and got all sulky. He's being a total butthead about it," Millie added. Mia and Millie looked at each other and just shrugged.

Before the conversation could continue, someone spilled a drink, and the girls moved onto another conversation.

A loud knock on the door was followed by their coach telling them fifteen minutes until lights out and it was time for everyone to get into their own rooms. Everyone said goodnight and filtered out until only Mia and Millie were left sitting in the room.

"Look, Mills, Cam told me what's going on, and I don't blame you for being upset at him. He's just being stupid, and I told him so."

"I know, right? I just don't understand boys sometimes," Millie replied.

"You'll be fine. Both of you. Look, I have to go to bed, but don't worry about Cameron. I'm sure he'll be fine. Goodnight, Mills."

"Thanks, Mia, same to you. Night." The girls hugged and Mia left for her own room. Millie spent a little while cleaning up the girls' mess before plugging her phone into its charger and crawling under the blankets.

Fifteen minutes later, a text message came in from Cameron apologizing for how he had been acting. Unfortunately, Millie had shut her eyes and fallen asleep within minutes.

Cameron stared at his phone for over an hour, waiting to see Millie's reply to his text before he put his own phone away angrily. He had tried to apologize and reach out, but it was clear Millie wasn't interested at all.

10

THE IMPROVISED FOYER/BREAKFAST area of the hotel was packed as all the kids and their parents started their busy day with a large and noisy breakfast. Millie scooted into a seat at a table with Georgia and some of the other girls from her team. *At least it wasn't as crowded as it was yesterday*, she thought as she mixed her fruit and yogurt together.

"So, you're not going to believe what happened to me in the elevator!" Georgia blurted out as they all ate their breakfast. In typical Georgia style, she didn't wait for anyone to answer before she just plowed into her story. "He's soooooo cute! He plays for the Blue Devils."

"What position?" one of the other girls asked, finally managing to get a word in.

"Well, he plays right wing, he has two sisters, loves pizza and chocolate, and he has the dreamiest eyes. Oh yeah, his name is Greyson. I almost forgot that!"

"OMG, Georgia. This hotel only has five floors. How long were you in there with him?"

"Well, we went up and down a few times!" Georgia replied sheepishly, before all the girls burst out laughing and giggling.

Cameron and some of the other boys from his team were sitting at another table as close as they could get to the girls in the crowed breakfast area. When they heard the girls laughing and giggling, all the boys turned to see what was so funny.

Cameron was trying to lock eyes with Millie, but she hadn't even looked at him. She still hadn't even responded to the text message he'd sent her last night. So much for being the bigger person.

"Rhys! What have I told you about being silly with your food?" Rhys' mom yelled out as she spotted her son flicking food across the table at one of his teammates.

"Seriously, Mom. You're embarrassing me," Rhys whined back while all the other boys started laughing.

"Really? You don't even know how embarrassing

I can get, young man. Now stop messing around and eat your breakfast already!"

"Sorry, Mom," Rhys said quietly, not even daring to look up and make eye contact with the rest of the boys who were almost crying they were laughing so hard. "Guys. Shut. Up." This only caused them to laugh even harder, with Cameron almost spitting his breakfast all over the table.

Millie caught movement out of the corner of her eye as someone walked into the breakfast room. She looked up to see Liam smiling at her as he walked in. He gave her a small wave, and Millie waved back, blushing as the other girls all started to "oooh" and "aaah" at her.

The coaches waited by the door, looking around before making eye contact with both captains and tapping their fingers on their watches to signal it was time to go. Millie and Cameron nodded, then told their teammates it was time to head out. At that, everyone shoved the last of their breakfast in before noisily clearing their tables. Before they could leave and head for the arena, they all needed to pack their bags and check out of their rooms with their parents.

Millie was quietly packing her bags when her mom walked into her room.

"So, who was that cute boy I saw you waving at downstairs?" she asked her daughter.

"Oh, you saw that, huh?"

"What boy?!" Millie's dad said, bursting out of the bathroom much more dramatically than the situation warranted.

"Dad, seriously," Millie said with a large sigh. Her dad was overly protective of her, but at the same time, it made her feel loved that her dad cared so much about her. "I just met him. You'd think I was planning on running away and marrying him the way the boys from our team are all acting."

"Marry?!" Millie and her mom heard her dad shout from the bathroom.

"Seriously, Mills, you're going to give your dad a heart attack." Her mom laughed. "Now, get packing so we can check out already."

Millie and her mom finished getting ready and piled all their gear near the front door. Between the hockey bags, coolers, food, and bags, there was a lot to pack up. Just as they were ready to leave, Millie's dad did a final walk-through of all the rooms to make sure they hadn't forgotten anything.

"Well, you're lucky I did a final check, miss,"

Millie's dad said, holding up her phone and charger in his hand.

"Thanks, Dad. You're a lifesaver. Can you put it in mom's bag? I won't need it until after the game anyway." Millie still hadn't noticed there was a message from Cameron flashing on the phone.

The bus ride to the arena was subdued, with most of the boys and girls more preoccupied with the upcoming game than messing around like usual when they were on the bus.

Tyler, the boys' trainer, was taking both teams to their warm-up so the girls could get ready and watch the boys' game before they went to play theirs. With Cameron and Millie not speaking yet, the other kids were starting to notice a lot of tension between their captains.

After both teams finished stretching, Millie stayed behind to ask Tyler to help show her how to stretch out the back of her leg as it had been giving her trouble over the weekend. Tyler showed her a few tricks to loosen up her leg and was just finishing when Millie noticed Liam was standing and watching her.

"Hey, good luck today, Liam," Millie said as the pair headed toward Liam's dressing room.

"Thanks, Millie. Same to you." Just as Liam was about to head toward the door to his dressing room, Cameron stuck his head out of his changing room and saw Liam and Millie talking to each other.

Typical, he thought, slamming the locker room door and slumping down on the bench. *Why couldn't she just hang out with one of the boys from her own town? Why did she have to be hanging out with the other team? And why hadn't she even bothered to text me back last night?*

"Seriously, dude. What's up? You look pissed off," Hunter asked.

"Nothing. I just need to focus on this game. We need to win this one for Link."

"Cam's right!" Hunter shouted as he stood up on the bench. "We need to win this one for Linkin! He broke his arm for this team, now we need to win this tournament for him!" The rest of the boys all chanted, "Link! Link! Link!"

Millie and Liam turned when they heard hockey sticks banging and the shouts of "Link! Link! Link!" coming from the other locker room.

"Wow. They're getting pretty psyched up in there, Millie," Liam said, sounding a little worried.

"Yep. Link broke his arm yesterday, and the boys are pretty angry about it. Anyways, good luck, Liam."

"Thanks, Millie, same to you. See you on the other side!" Liam said as he walked away.

11

THE NERVES AND tension were building in the dressing room as all the boys went through their pregame routines. Some were quiet and subdued, deep in thought, while others were bouncing off the walls. Throughout all of this, their favorite pregame music mix was pumping from a Bluetooth stereo sitting in the corner.

Coach John and the other coaches stood in front of a large whiteboard sketching out plays at one end of the dressing room.

"Okay, boys, quiet down and all eyes on me for a minute!" Coach John shouted. Someone turned down the music while the rest of the boys sat down and focused on the coach. "We have the skills to beat these guys, but it's about who wants it more. The only person standing in your way is you. If you guys *all* show up to play from start to finish, then I don't think they stand a chance. This means every faceoff is ours, we always get to the puck first, we always have a man in front of our net, and everyone plays together." The boys all banged their sticks on the ground. They wanted this, and they would win it.

"Oh, and just in case anyone forgot, we're a man down. That means we'll be running with three defense, and if it's not running well, we'll double shift the centers. For now, we're just going to play it by ear and see what happens. Short shifts, 30 to 40 seconds max, and you're off. I have no problem sitting out anyone who plays selfish. We're a team, and we'll only win by playing as one!" The boys all cheered and clapped. They knew this tournament was only one game away from being theirs.

"I spoke to Linkin's dad, and Linkin is going to be joining you guys on the bench and helping us out through the game. So, make sure you remember who we're playing for."

"And no stupid penalties!" Logan blurted out.

"Exactly! We can't afford to be another player down. Being on a penalty kill could easily cost us this game. Okay, Cameron, can you count them down? Let's do this boys!" Coach John added.

"Lightning on three: one...two...three!" Cam shouted.

"LIGHTNING!" all the boys screamed.

This was it. The final game of the tournament. One more win and they'd be taking home not only the trophy, but also the glory.

As the two teams were warming up on the ice, the arena stands began to fill up with spectators from both teams and other people at the tournament waiting for their games later that day.

The Hurricanes' parents were in the stands with the Lightning parents. Some of the siblings had put up their banners and were patiently waiting for the game to begin so they'd have an opportunity to ring their cow bells.

The girls had all left their change room and taken up a spot around the glass walls of the arena where they'd be able to watch the game while still standing on the rubber mats protecting their skates.

A piercing wail from the buzzer announced their warm-up time was over, and it was almost time to begin the game. Both teams spent a few seconds clearing the ice of the pucks they'd been using for their warm-up and headed to center ice where they lined up ready to shake hands or bump gloves.

Both Cameron and Liam were lined up right behind their goalies at the front of their team's line, a look of determination etched on their faces. Millie noticed there was a slight pause as Cam and Liam came up beside each other. *Please let this go well*, Millie thought.

Cam reached out with his glove and gave Liam a fist bump as Liam fist bumped him back, and the two players locked eyes with each other. They paused for what felt like an eternity.

"You guys are going down," Cam said flatly as if the outcome of the game was already a forgone conclusion.

"Game on, bro," winked Liam.

Cam didn't show it, but Liam's response made him angrier than he knew it should have. He continued down the line and skated back to the bench with an angry expression across his face.

"Dude, you seriously have to just let it go already," Hunter said seeing the look on Cam's face. "The best way to get to this guy is to just get even. We're going to kick their butt all over this

ice, and let everyone know who the best team in this tournament is."

Cameron smiled at Hunter's words, and for a second, forgot all about Liam. The guys on the ice lined up against the boards and, as one, screamed "Lightning!"

The first faceoff of the game saw the two rivals, Liam and Cameron, lined up against each other on center ice. They were both bent over the puck, staring each other down.

The referee signaled both goalies to make sure they were ready, holding the puck in position above the boys' sticks, ready to drop it.

He dropped the puck. Liam won it and sent it sliding back toward his defense. They picked it up cleanly and tried to move the puck up through the center of the ice, but they were stopped cold by the Lightning defense.

Then a change of possession saw the Lighting heading over the red line. Luke fired the puck down the side of the ice deep into the Blue Devils' end. Hunter was already heading down the opposite side of the ice, hoping that he'd be able to outskate the defensemen frantically trying to chase down the flying puck.

Cameron and Luke headed for the net but

ended up getting tangled in their haste to make it. Just as they managed to get themselves sorted out, they looked up to see Hunter had won his race to the puck and was already moving into position to pass it to one of his teammates. When he saw no players open in front of the net, he passed it into space, hoping someone could break free and take possession.

Cam was ready, but so was Liam. He pushed Cam off balance before intercepting the puck and skating up the ice. Then Liam passed to one of the players just coming off the bench with fresh legs. As the Blue Devils headed up the ice, the Lighting offense got caught deep and were struggling to get back, leaving their defensemen to hold up the Blue Devils.

The Blue Devils passed the puck around in the Lightening end. A quick pass by the offense and a slap shot on goal was easily saved by Logan in net.

The first period was almost over, with the puck going back and forth as neither team was able to slide it past the goalies, both of whom were on fire making some awesome saves. There were only forty-five seconds left on the clock when Liam managed to collect the puck and get a breakaway after a slapshot by Ben bounced off Liam's pads.

Cameron was right behind him, with both players finding themselves on the same line rotation, and catching up fast as Liam headed up the ice. Liam risked a quick look behind him. He knew Cam was the faster skater, but Liam also knew he had better stick-handling skills.

Liam took a chance and slowed slightly so Cameron ended up beside him. This move caught Cam off guard, allowing Liam the room he needed to drive forward and dangle around him. The net was coming up fast, and he knew it was now or never if he was going to take the shot.

The shot was perfect! It flew past Logan, who was desperately trying to reach it at full stretch, and into the back of the net.

Cameron skid to a stop, smashing his stick down on the ice angrily. "Damn it!" he spat out angrily.

Liam skated over to the rest of his line, who were already fist pumping and clapping each other on the back. Then he headed over to his bench, and on the way, he spotted Millie watching him through the glass. He gave her a little wave, hoping no one else noticed.

Cameron was heading back to his own bench when he saw Liam wave, so he looked in the direction Liam was waving. *Damn it, now she's waving at the guy when he scores on the Lightning?* The siren sounded and both teams headed to their benches.

"Okay, guys, this isn't the start we hoped for, and frankly, you've only got yourself to blame. Remember, we're not playing their game; we're playing our game. So, let's get our act together and play it the Lightning way!"

Cameron waited impatiently for his line to be called so he could get back on the ice. They needed to get it back. It wasn't going down like this. Not today. He was angry at himself for not stopping Liam when he'd had the chance and falling for that trick move. He should have gotten the puck from Liam, and now they were down a goal.

The Blue Devils were heading up the ice as the doors opened to signal it was time for Cam to hit the ice. Straight away, he found himself on the wrong side of a bad change. He headed into the corner to try and help Ben out because he was jammed up in the corner with Liam and another Blue Devil player all over him like a rash.

Cameron found himself trading stick blows with Liam, which quickly escalated into the pair shoving each other. Cam pushed a little harder than Liam, sending him flying over a player's stick and crashing into the ice. A whistle from the referee stopped play and saw Cam heading toward the penalty box with a roughing call.

Cameron slammed the penalty box door and lost his temper completely. He knew he was better than this, but he just couldn't seem to get his head together. Hunter skated past his captain and gave him a mocking applause, shaking his head in disgust.

As Cam looked up at the scoreboard, he saw Mia frowning at him from behind the glass. The dirty look on Millie's face wasn't much better.

Somehow, the Lightning managed to keep the puck out of their net with some amazing defense from the penalty kill line during the penalty.

When the time on his penalty ended, Cameron jumped out of the penalty box and headed over to his bench. When Cam reached the bench, Coach John pulled him to one side as far away as possible from the other players on the bench.

"Do we have a problem, Cam?" Coach John asked quietly. Whenever he was really angry, he got eerily quiet and calm, like a wild dog about to attack.

"No, coach. It won't happen again. I just got carried away there. Sorry."

"Actually, what it looks like is that this whole game, you have had an issue with number sixteen. I don't know what it is, and to be honest I really don't care. Get your head in the game, or I will sit you out, and they'll win or lose while you watch. Down or not, the selfish crap ends right now. It's impacting the team. Snap out of it or take a seat."

"Yes, coach," Cam said quietly. He knew he was letting the team down.

The rest of the second period saw both teams battle back and forth with no goals on either side.

The Lighting were heading into the last period of the game one goal down, and they were running out of steam. They knew it and the Blue Devils could sense it like sharks when there's blood in the water. They were circling.

Preston headed out onto the ice to team up with Taylor. They were going to try running with two centers for the rest of the game. There wasn't much time left, and something had to happen.

Cameron knew it was now or never, and he had to get his butt in gear and his head in the game.

Cameron pushed all thoughts of Liam and

Millie aside and dropped the hammer. He knew they needed a goal and they needed it now.

Rhys was heading up the ice with one of the Blue Devils' wingers hooking him from behind. Rhys was desperately trying to fight him off and keep hold of the puck, but the situation was getting desperate.

He frantically tried to deke out of the way, but the winger's stick took his skates out from under him, and Rhys crashed hard into the boards. Cameron was a split second behind and in the perfect position to nab the loose puck before the defenseman had a chance to gather it up. The referee raised his arm, ready to blow the whistle if the Lightning lost possession of the puck.

"Logan! Bench!" Coach John screamed at his goalie. He wanted that extra player on the ice but couldn't do it until Logan made it to the bench. Logan skated like his life depended on it toward the bench.

Cam and Hunter headed into the Blue Devils' end and desperately tried to keep possession of the puck to give the rest of their team time to get set up. The Blue Devils were trying anything to touch the puck and force the referee to blow the whistle.

The Blue Devils were breathing hard, while Cameron, Preston, and Ben played pass the puck. It had already been a long shift, and there was no way they were getting off the ice until this all unfolded.

Millie and the rest of the girls from the Hurricanes were banging their sticks and hands against the glass.

"This is the most exciting game of monkey in the middle I've ever seen!" Khloe screamed.

The clock was slowly ticking down, and the Lighting needed a goal desperately to level the score. It seemed as if the entire Lighting team had taken the ice, and the Blue Devils just couldn't get that puck.

Cam saw the moment he had been waiting for and broke free from the passing back and forth and headed toward the net. Rhys skated backwards toward the goalie, screening him as Cameron headed in, and Preston and Ben moved around the Blue Devils' defensemen.

A quick pass from Ben to Preston gave Preston the opportunity to wind up for a big shot on net. Liam and the other defensemen saw him winding up and stood tall, hoping to block the shot. At the last second, Preston flicked it back to Ben who passed it to Cameron.

Cameron flicked the puck at the net and watched as it bounced off Rhys' stick before clipping the goalie's pads and sliding off its intended path. Hunter was right there waiting and quickly scooped it toward the net. The goalie tried desperately to recover but only ended up getting tangled up with Rhys.

Goal! The entire team skated over to Hunter, jumping, clapping, and screaming. Half the arena was on their feet, and cowbells were clanging as parents and children clapped and cheered.

Coach John signaled a timeout as the players headed toward the bench.

"Nice teamwork, boys. It's about time. Now, we've got two minutes left, and this game isn't going to overtime. Cameron is going to win the faceoff, and then you're going to drive hard up the center of the ice. You can do this. If you do it as a team. Now, go win this for Linkin."

Cameron was tired as he headed back out to the center for the faceoff, but there was no way he was missing this. Liam, his face bright red, skated up and faced off against Cam. Cameron noticed Liam wasn't as chirpy as he had been at the start of the game, and he didn't seem to be moving as easily either.

The referee dropped the puck, and Cameron easily won it, flicking it toward Hunter as the pair started smashing their way up toward the Blue Devils' net. Liam was desperately trying to get into a position to head off Cameron as one of the Blue Devils' defensemen attacked Hunter. As another defensemen joined the battle for the puck, Hunter flicked it to Cameron.

Cameron got the puck and put his head down as he charged up the ice. Liam was trying to skate backwards while using his stick to knock the puck away from Cam, but his tired arms and legs weren't working as quickly as they had been.

Cam deked around Liam. Now it was just open ice between him and the Blue Devils' goalie: a one-versus-one battle between him and the goalie. Cameron already knew this was going to be the winning goal—it had to be.

The seconds were ticking down as he barreled down on the goalie. Cam deked to the left before switching the puck back to the right, his strongest side. He wound up for the shot and unloaded one of the most powerful shots of his life.

The puck sailed straight past the goalie's

outstretched hand and into the back of the net! Cameron skated past on one leg, fist pumping the air as the rest of the Lighting piled on top of him.

They all skated back to their bench as the team erupted into cheers, smashing their sticks against the boards. There were only forty-five seconds left on the clock, and the Blue Devils were exhausted.

The crowd around the arena was still cheering as Preston lined up for the faceoff. All they had to do was keep possession for the remainder of the game, and this game was theirs!

Preston won the faceoff, and he and Hunter moved the puck forward slowly and carefully as the seconds ticked down. When the buzzer sounded to signal the end of the game, the Lightening threw their gloves and sticks into the air as the entire team hit the ice for the biggest pile up ever seen.

The Lightening had won the game and the tournament. It was up to the girls now to take the win and give them both a reason to celebrate.

12

THE ARENA WAS filled with loud cheering and screaming from all the Lightning and Hurricane families. Millie was beaming and banging on the boards, along with the other Hurricane girls.

"They played a strong game, but that was way too close if you ask me," Sage mumbled to no one in particular in between cheering and clapping for the boys' team.

"Yes, I agree. But we need to get to our dressing room and get ready ourselves," Millie said looking up and down the line of girls half-dressed in an assortment of hockey equipment and uniforms. "Hey! Let's go, guys. We can see the photos later."

The Hurricanes headed into their dressing room to get the rest of their hockey gear on. Just a few minutes later, Coach Phil knocked then walked in for their pregame pep talk.

"Ladies, settle down and listen up. I know you all know how important this game is. So, I won't go on too long, but you guys met some great competition this weekend, and every time you kept pushing and came out on top, no matter what they threw at you. We might not be the biggest team out there, but you girls are definitely one of the fastest. You have so much heart and skill it's amazing to watch you all carve it up out there. Remember, play your game. Don't get caught up with the penalties and fall into the trap of playing it their way. I've checked around, and this team has a reputation for playing rough. So, keep your heads up and play smart. Let's bring home this trophy."

"Who are we?" Millie shouted as she stepped forward into the middle of the dressing room.

"Hurricanes!" the girls all shouted back.

"Who are we?!" Millie screamed back.

"Hurricanes!" they all hollered while jumping up and down.

Khloe led them out of the dressing room toward the ice. The boys had all waited so they could line up outside the girls' change room for fist pumps and high fives as the girls headed out onto the ice.

Millie walked along the line until she found herself facing Cameron. They locked eyes.

"Good luck, Millie," Cam said quietly.

"Thanks," Millie mumbled back, not quite making eye contact.

The girls all hit the ice just as the pregame music kicked off. It was always a good sign when they had some music to get them pumped up before a game. The Hornets were warming up on the other half of the ice. *Wow! They are big*, Millie noticed as she went through her usual warm-up routine while also checking out the other team.

Then the arena buzzer went off, loudly signaling it was time to get the game started. Millie skated over to get in position and adjusted her mouthguard. She locked eyes with Mia on the bench, and the pair nodded at each other. It was go time.

Back in the change room, the boys were all rushing to get their gear off as fast as possible so they could hit the showers and get dressed. Boys being boys, most of them would have preferred to skip the shower, but their parents and coaches had already warned them that if they didn't shower, they could find their own way home!

There was a lot of laughing and cheering still

going on in the dressing room. Their spirits still high from taking out the tournament. The dressing room looked like a tornado had gone through, with hockey equipment and clothes strewn everywhere. There were only three shower stalls in the change room, so it was a mad dash to see who could get in and out first.

Even with the superfast showers and changing, the girls were already up 1-0 by the time all the boys had cleared the dressing room and found a good spot to watch the game. There were only a few minutes left in the first period.

Neither team had been able to add another score to the board when the buzzer sounded to signal the end of the first period. It was still 1-0 as the girls skated over to the bench.

"Great first period, girls. Now, we need to get some more scores on the board. Make sure you're looking for those rebounds. Their goalie is good, but she's letting a lot of rebounds back on the ice, and we're not taking advantage of them. Mia, nice pass to Daylyn, and Daylyn, that was a great shot from the point. Keep it up. If we get a chance to feed our defense the puck, do it, but make sure you crowd the goalie. Screen her and then look for the rebounds."

The girls all stood quietly while Coach Phil spoke to them, using the break to drink from their bottles and rehydrate before the next period. After he finished talking, the girls did a quick cheer, and then the second period was under way.

Within a few minutes, it was clear they weren't playing with the same intensity they had during the first period. The break seemed to have slowed down the momentum they'd had going into the first period.

"We can't seem to get the puck out of our end this period!" exclaimed Millie, breathing hard.

"You're not wrong! I'm glad Khloe is on fire. We'd be toast if she wasn't. We have to figure this out before this game gets out of control!" Georgia replied as the two girls looked up at where the other team was preparing to launch another push forward.

No sooner had the words left her mouth than one of the Hornets' forwards flew up the boards and sent a cross-ice pass to one of their players. The Hurricanes were caught off guard and could only watch as she slapped a hard shot into Khloe. The puck bounced off Khloe's pads but was quickly scooped up by the one of the Hornets, who fired it straight back to her teammate on the opposite side of the goal. Khloe was an awesome goalie, but the three quick changes in direction were too much for her. Caught off balance, the Hornets slipped the puck into the net.

The Hurricanes headed toward the bench with their heads down. Now the score was tied 1-1 in the middle of the second.

Coach Phil, seeing the expression and body language of his players as they skated toward him, knew he needed to switch things up.

"Ref! Time out!" he yelled, making the timeout signal with his hands. Khloe heard the timeout call and skated over to join her teammates on the bench.

"Look, girls, I don't know what happened, but snap out of it. This is our game. Not theirs! Khloe, you're playing amazingly. Don't change anything. Even the best goalies in the NHL get scored on."

Khloe nodded and seemed to puff herself up a little bit. No goalie ever liked being scored on, and it was easy to fall into the trap of blaming yourself.

Coach Phil continued, "We've lost our momentum, but we're going to get it back. It's been a physical game so far, but we're going to go back out there and show them what real hockey skills are. Now, we're going to mix things up a bit, so just go with the flow."

The girls looked at each other, a little confused and curious about what was about to happen. Their coach always seemed to have an idea to help them out when they needed it most.

"We're going to switch the lines up a little. Millie, I want you to play with Keira and Maddie. Mia, you're going to play with Georgia and Violet. Isabella, you'll be playing with Lola and Sage." Coach Phil raised his hands defensively, preempting the comments and questions he knew were about to be thrown his way. "I know this is a bit odd, but you've all played together in practices, and I want to see how it goes."

The juniors getting an opportunity to step up looked at each other with shocked and excited expressions. Nervous smiles were plastered all over their faces. The seniors looked at each other and shrugged, just accepting the changes without comment. They knew something had to change if they wanted to take back control of this game.

There were only eight minutes left of the second period when Millie's line headed back out onto the ice.

The boys watching from around the boards noticed straight away something was different.

"Is Millie playing with two juniors, Cam?" whispered Logan.

"Yeah? That's totally weird. I wonder what's going on?" Cameron wasn't sure why Coach Phil would make such a drastic change, especially putting so many juniors in, but the girls had seemed to struggle during the second period.

Millie dominated the faceoff, passing the puck back to Ashlyn, who quickly worked the puck over to her twin, Daylyn, on the other side of the ice. Daylyn took a quick look down the ice and spotted Maddie, who had just done a quick pivot to get away from her winger and was heading into a clearing. Daylyn fired off a hard pass toward where she thought Maddie would be in a second's time. Maddie got the puck and stepped over the blue line, heading hard to the net. She could see Millie and Keira right beside. Keira pushed hard and headed deep. Maddie saw her stick and passed the puck. It found Keira's stick. Keira one timed it, and it flew deep into the net. Goal! The arena erupted with cheering, cowbells, and boys banging on the boards around the ice. The girls all skated over to Keira and gave her a big group hug.

The girls lined up again and got ready to do it all over again. Within a few minutes, it was clear the girls have wrestled the momentum back from the Hornets.

Mia's line was on the ice when she was tripped by one of the Hornets in what was clear to everyone as an intentional penalty. The referee saw it and blew her whistle, stopping the play and sending the guilty player to the penalty box for a two-minute penalty.

Normally, Coach Phil would switch up his lines and send the power-play line out, but this time, he decided to wait and see what this new line could do. He wasn't disappointed!

Within thirty seconds of the play commencing, Mia and Georgia used their speed and agility to cut through the Hornets' defense. Mia smashed a shot in on the startled goalie, the puck bouncing back off her pads to where Violet was swooping in. She gathered the puck and did a fast backhand shot over the goalie's shoulder and into the net for their third goal!

With only a few seconds left in the second period, the scores were now 3-1 in favor of the Hurricanes.

"We've got this! Keep it up!" Millie shouted

from the bench where she and the rest of the team were on their feet, banging their sticks against the boards.

The girls lined up for the faceoff, but within a few seconds, the siren blared, signaling the end of the second period.

After another water stop and a quick pep talk from Coach Phil, the girls took the ice for the third and final period. Isabella led the girls for this line. She was a fantastic player but was quiet and shy, which usually prevented Coach Phil from seeing her full potential unleashed on the ice.

Well, not this time! One of the Hornets skated over and took out Lola almost as soon as the play started. Isabella was the first into the fray, helping Lola to her feet before unleashing on the other player. The referee wasn't far behind, sending the Hornets' player to the penalty box for another two-minute roughing penalty.

"Thanks!" Lola said to Isabella, patting the usually quiet girl on the back.

"You're welcome," Isabella replied, blushing with embarrassment at the compliment.

The third period saw most of the plays going the Hurricanes' way. They managed to keep the puck in the Hornets' end of the ice but failed to add to the 3-1 score.

Now there were only three minutes left in the game, and the Hurricanes were pushing hard for another goal to cement their lead and the win. Three minutes left on the clock means a lot can still happen in a hockey game. No one was getting comfortable, and the girls weren't taking their eyes off the prize.

A bad change by the Hurricanes gave the Hornets the opportunity they'd been waiting for. Their offense seized the puck and powered up the ice on a breakaway. The Hurricanes' defense were scrambling to get the puck, but the other girl was just too far ahead.

Khloe was shuffling slowly side to side in her crease, her eyes never leaving the player as the Hornets' player bore down on her. Khloe was as ready as she'd ever be.

The Hornets' player tried to deke her, but Khloe had anticipated the move and took a chance. Khloe poke checked her, knocking the puck backwards onto the ice. Within a heartbeat, Khloe was back in her stance and ready for whatever happened next.

Daylyn, barreling down on the action unfolding in front of her, swooped in and scooped up the

puck heading back toward the other end of the ice. The crowd was on their feet chanting, "Go low, go low," from the stands. Khloe turned slowly and raised her stick in the air, acknowledging the chant before taking a drink and getting back into position.

There was only one minute left on the clock when Coach Phil used his last time out to give everyone a water break and put a fresh line on the ice.

Millie's line took the ice, and she'd already anticipated what was going to unfold next. As soon as the Hornets moved the puck into the Hurricanes' end, their goalie headed to the bench, and a sixth player jumped onto the ice.

As the seconds slowly ticked down, it became a brutal defense game as the girls threw every trick they knew into keeping the Hornets from getting into a position to score. Millie wrestled the puck away on the boards but soon found herself pinned, with the Hornets' players slashing away at her legs and stick, desperately trying to get at the puck. Kiera rushed into help as loud cheering erupted around the arena.

The buzzer sounded loudly, cutting through the cheers. The Hurricanes' bench emptied as all the girls skated toward their goalie, Khloe, jumping on her and sending her crashing down onto the ice.

"Don't crush her!" Millie shouted loudly. "She's the best goalie ever, and it would be a pain in the butt to replace her now!" The girls laughed and hugged each other as they all celebrated an awesome win.

It's not always the team with the biggest players that wins, Millie grinned. *Sometimes it's the team with the biggest heart.*

Both teams lined up to receive their medals, with the Hurricanes also receiving a large tournament trophy. The boys were all lined up against the glass cheering and clapping.

Millie received her medal and waved to the cheering parents crowding around trying to take photos. She looked up into the stands and noticed Liam was clapping and waving. *I can't believe he stayed behind to watch the whole game*, she thought happily. She gave him a shy little wave before lining back up with her teammates.

Cameron followed Millie's wave and also saw Liam clapping and waving. *I suppose it was pretty cool of the guy to hang around just to support the Hurricanes after he'd just lost his own game*, he decided. *The guy can't be all that bad. Even if he does play for someone else.*

After a second's hesitation, he pushed himself off the glass he'd been standing against. *It's about time I made this right,* Cameron thought and started walking toward Liam. It was time he acted his age and settled this silly act he'd been putting on for Millie's sake. It sucked not being able to hang out and have a laugh with his best friend.

It was time he stopped being a jerk.

Millie stopped mid-clap as she saw Cam heading toward Liam.

"Wow! Wish I could be a fly on the wall for that conversation!" Georgia said, following the direction of Millie's eyes. Millie looked at Mia—who looked up to see Cam closing the distance on Liam—and shrugged. Mia shrugged back, both of them confused about what was going on in the stands.

"Millie, Georgia, and Daylyn! Get up here!" Coach Phil shouted from the front where he was holding the large trophy.

All three girls skated over, and together, they lifted the cup up over their heads. Then they all headed down to the net to take their team photos.

In the stands, Liam finally noticed Cameron

closing in on him. The pair of boys looked at each other cautiously as they squared off.

"Look, I've been acting like an idiot all weekend. I wanted to apologize to you face to face. My dad always taught me you need to face your problems, not run away from them." Liam went to say something, but Cameron held up his hands, interrupting. "Before you say anything, I'm not a hundred percent convinced about you, but Millie is my best friend, and I'm sure she sees something in you I obviously don't. But if you hurt her, you'll have me and the rest of those boys out there to answer to. Okay?"

"I don't have any plans to hurt her. I'm not even sure what our plans are. All I know is she's a cool girl, and I just wanted to get to know her."

"No worries. We're both on the same page then," Cam replied, extending his hand. "Peace?"

"Peace," Liam said reaching out with own hand and shaking Cameron's hand.

Mia and Millie watched the exchange from down on the ice.

"Well, well. Looks like someone's gotten over whatever was bothering him," Millie said to her friend.

"I knew he would. Just takes those boys a little longer to figure it out sometimes."

Both girls laughed and giggled as they focused on getting their photos taken.

13

ALL THE PLAYERS had piled onto the team's bus, most of them listening to music and relaxing after their big wins.

Millie was busy texting back and forth with Liam.

After the game, Liam had found her before she had got changed and congratulated her on an awesome game. Millie had blushed bright red. She wasn't used to all the attention. Liam had said he would love to keep in touch and slipped her his phone number before apologizing for having to leave so soon. His parents had been nice enough to let him stay and watch, but they were waiting in the parking lot to leave.

Within a few minutes of settling into the bus ride, Millie had sent her first text to Liam.

"Attention!" Coach John shouted from the front

of the bus where he was standing with Coach Phil. "We aren't going to talk long, but we wanted to say how proud of you we all are. You did a fantastic job, and we couldn't have asked for a better bunch of kids."

"Coach John is right. Great job all! Enjoy this week, but remember we have practice Tuesday!" This got the round of groans the coaches had expected. "Seriously, great job everyone. Now, relax and enjoy the ride home," Coach Phil said before sitting down next to Janet, his team manager.

"Look at that!" Georgia said, excitedly pointing at where Coach Phil and Janet were laughing and chatting away together at the front of the bus.

"Girl! They are so in love!" Khloe blurted out.

"Guys, seriously. Gross," Daylyn replied.

"Yeah, enough already," Ashlyn chimed in.

"Coach Phil is going to be your new dad! Coach Phil is going to be your new dad!" Khloe was quietly singing away, much to the twins' horror.

Meanwhile, Mia had swapped seats and slipped in quietly next to Millie, who appeared to be engrossed in her phone.

"Who ya texting?" Mia asked, despite already having guessed the answer.

"Umm, Liam. My mom is letting me use her hotspot." Millie was blushing again. *Get it together girl*, she said to herself. *You can't go bright red every time you mention his name.*

"Thought so! Anyway, Cam told me what he and Liam talked about in the stands. Cam's cool and he's sorry he acted like a spoiled brat," Mia said to Millie.

"I know. Liam told me. I got Cam's text from last night too, just before we got on the bus, and had a chat with him. I'm glad we're all okay again."

"Me too!" Mia said reaching over to hug Millie.

"So, what's going to happen with you and Liam?" Mia asked.

"Not sure. We haven't really talked about it. For now, we're just friends, and we'll see what happens I guess."

"Well, championships aren't far away. The way Liam's team played, they're going to make it for sure. You guys might be able to meet up again."

"I hope so. You never know what's going to happen in hockey though."

AVAILABLE NOW

Made in the USA
San Bernardino, CA
26 January 2020